W9-DBX-437

2-24-05

ABDO Publishing Company is the exclusive school and library distributor of Rabbit Ears Books.

Library bound edition 2005.

Copyright © 1995 Rabbit Ears Productions, Inc.,
Rowayton, Connecticut.

Library of Congress Cataloging-in-Publication Data

Metaxas, Eric.
 Mose the Fireman / written by Eric Metaxas ; illustrated by Everett Peck.
     p. cm.
 "Rabbit Ears books."
 Summary: Relates the tall tale adventures of Mose Humphries, a nineteenth-century
fireman in New York City.
 ISBN 1-59197-766-5
 [1. Fire fighters—Fiction. 2. New York (N.Y.)—Fiction. 3. Tall tales.] I. Peck Everett,
ill. II. Title.

PZ7.M564Mo 2004
[Fic]—dc22

                                                                    2004047728

All Rabbit Ears books are reinforced library binding
and manufactured in the United States of America.

Mose the Fireman

written by Eric Metaxas
illustrated by Everett Peck

Rabbit Ears Books

xcuse me. Excuse me. I hate to bother you, but I just wanted to ask you if by any chance you'd ever heard of a guy by the name of Mose the Fireman. Moses Humphries was his real name, and he was the greatest firefighter who ever lived. This is going way back now. In fact, this goes so far back, New York City was so new that it still had a price tag on it. But seriously, this is a long, long time ago. It's even before subways were invented.

Now, to begin at the beginning, Mose Humphries was born in 1809 in a tenement on the Lower East Side of New York City, the same year Abraham Lincoln was born in a log cabin on the plains of Illinois. Anyhow, that winter there was a big fire in New York. Every fireman in the city was trying to put it out. It burned all through the night, destroying block after block of wooden houses. It was very sad. You see, they didn't have too many fireplugs at that time, so they had to pump the water right out of whatever river or pond or pothole was close by.

Anyhow, just as they were putting out the last fire, there was a big explosion—*ba-boom!*—that blasted the top half of a building into a million pieces.

Now, most of it landed in the icy waters of the East River, and everyone who had been trapped inside was given up for dead. But not long after that one of the firemen from Engine Company Number 40 heard a cry from down by the river, and right there lying in a busted hogshead among the frozen cattails they found a little redheaded baby.

Well, the firemen of Number 40 decided to adopt the little guy right then and there, and because of the way they'd found him they decided to name him Moses after the guy who was also found floating in a river, although not in the East River and not in New York. And so Moses it was, although practically everybody just called him Mose.

And so Mose grew up in a firehouse. He took his first bath inside a fire helmet. And they used a big coil of hose for his playpen.

Now, as you already know, fire fighting was a very primitive operation back in the old days. To begin with, they had only one piece of equipment, called an engine, which was really just a big, clunky water pump on wheels. And because all the firemen were volunteers in those days, whenever the fire bell sounded they would all stop whatever they were doing, run to the firehouse, haul the old engine out, and then they'd drag it to the fire themselves with ropes, which was no piece of cake. You see, it wasn't until many years later that they figured out they could get horses to do it. These guys were not exactly valedictorians.

Pretty soon they'd let Mose ride to the fire with them. He'd watch as the fire marshal shouted orders to everybody through a silver speaking trumpet. "Man the brakes!" the marshal would say. The brakes were the big handles that pumped the water. "Man the brakes! Watch that hose there! Step lively, boys! Can the mongoose!"

And the men would pump up and down on the brakes as fast as they could, and this would suck the water out of the wooden pipes that ran along most of the main roads and shoot it out the other end. It was hard work.

ell, Mose grew up fast, and pretty soon he was right in there with them, hauling the engine. And not long after that, he was so big and strong that the men would just let him pull it all by himself. Now, the engine at Company Number 40 was called Lady Washington— that's George's wife—and there wasn't a more beautiful piece of equipment anywhere.

Whenever the fire bell sounded, Mose was always the first one ready to haul her off. You see, Mose was never one to fool around with stairs. He'd just throw his boots out the window and take a flying leap right after them, putting them on as he fell and landing without a hitch. It got to where he could jump out the window, shave, comb his hair, brush his teeth, eat some oatmeal, read three chapters of the Good Book, and drink some coffee—without spilling a drop! Mose was some kind of fireman.

Now, I wouldn't want to give you the idea that Mose and the Bowery
Boys of Company Number 40 were the only ones fighting fires in New
York. There were fire companies all over the city. And every company
thought their engine was the best, so I guess you could say they had a little
rivalry going on among them.

Whenever a fire alarm went off, three or four companies would all race
to the fire at once, hoping to be the one to tap the fireplug and have
the honor of holding the hose and putting out the fire.

One time two companies got into a brawl over a plug while the very fire they should have been putting out continued to burn.

Now Mose and Sykesey, who was Mose's best pal, couldn't believe what they were seeing. They had to do something.

"Who needs a fireplug, anyway!" Mose shouted. "C'mon, Sykesey, let's go!" So Mose grabbed a pickax and made a hole in the pipe itself. "Sykesey, take the butt!" he shouted.

Sykesey grabbed the nozzle and pointed it at the fire, and then Mose stuck the other end right into the hole he'd made in the water pipe and began pumping the engine brakes all by himself. The water shot out with such force that the fire was out in no time, and Sykesey had to hose down the brawling companies just so's he could tell 'em to go home. That cooled 'em off.

Now as you've probably already figured out, the Bowery was kind of a wacko place. There were live pigs running wild through the streets, rooting around to eat whatever scraps of food they could find, and wherever you turned there were chimney sweeps and vendors of all kinds selling onions and whatnot, and there were guys with carts that sold steaming hot yams and fresh apples and baked pears dripping with syrup. I'm getting hungry just thinking about it. Somebody run down and get me a cannoli!

And each of these characters would have a song that he would sing. Like the guy who sold clams would sing:

"My clams I want to sell today,
The best clams from Rock-a-way! Hey!"

But the most popular street food of them all was the boiled ears of corn that were carried in cedar buckets by the white-corn gals of the Bowery.

One day as Mose was swaggering down the Bowery with Sykesey, he spotted a white-corn gal named Lize. And it might be a corny way of putting it, but when she sang her voice was as sweet as the corn she sold.

"Hot corn! Hot corn!
Here's your lily-white corn.
All you that's got money,
Poor me that's got none.
Buy my lily-white corn,
And let me go home."

What an attitude! But hey, this is New York we're talking about. Besides, it sold corn, am I right?

Well, what can I say? Mose was gaga— head over heels in love. Now, the natural thing for a Bowery Boy to do when he was in love was to ask his gal to go to the fireman's ball with him, but somehow Mose just couldn't get up the nerve. You see, without some big, scary fire roaring around him, Mose was as shy as could be. And so he'd just buy some corn and be on his way.

Well, pretty soon the fireman's ball was right around the corner, and Mose still hadn't asked her. But lucky for Mose there was a big fire over on Delancey Street.

That was some blaze, all right. The flames shot way up over the top of a four-story building, which was the tallest building in New York at that time. And it presented some real problems for the firemen, because they didn't have ladders that could get up that high.

Mose was on the scene in a flash with the Bowery Boys of Number 40 right behind him. The building was covered in flames, and it looked like it was going to collapse any minute. Then all of a sudden they heard this voice calling for help.

And then Mose saw her, on the fourth floor, right through the burning flames! It was Lize, his white-corn gal.

Without even stopping to think, he ran over to a shipbuilder's joint and grabbed the tallest ship's mast he could find. Then, like the lunatic that he was, he sprinted toward the burning building and pole-vaulted right up to the fourth floor!

Well, what with all those flames roaring around him, Mose felt like his usual brave self, so then and there on the windowsill, with the building about to collapse and the fire so hot that they were both sweating bullets, Mose asked Lize if she'd go to the fireman's ball with him. Well, what's she gonna say? "I'd love to," she said. And that was that.

That's all Mose
needed to hear. He was so
happy, he couldn't
contain himself. He
grabbed Lize and was
just about to jump out
the window with her,
when he realized he should
probably do something a
little more civilized—
what with her being a real
lady and all—so holding onto
Lize with his right arm and the ship's
mast with the other, he slid all the
way down to the ground. It was a straight
shot, no traffic.

Oh, by the way,
that's how the fire pole
was invented. I'll bet you
didn't know that, did you?
You probably thought it was
Ben Franklin or Tom Edison who
invented it, didn't you? Well, it
was Mose who did it, and if
photography had been
popular then, I'd show
you pictures to prove it.

Well, it wasn't long before the fireman's ball rolled around. Mose got all gussied up for it—although no Bowery Boy ever went anywhere without wearing his red-flannel fire shirt. You see, you could never tell when there was going to be a fire, and you had to be prepared. But because of his love for Lize, Mose put a white dickey over the top of it—very classy. Of course, Lize didn't look so bad herself. She was a sight for sore eyes.

The two of them danced all through the night. It was Mose's dream come true.

Well, Mose wasn't one to waste time, and after a couple of hours of dancing with Lize, he was all set to propose marriage. That's all there was to it.

So he wiped his mouth on his sleeve and he cleared his throat. And he said, "Lize, will you m—"

But just as he was getting to the point, Mose heard a distant sound, a bell, coming from the direction of City Hall. Being the remarkable fireman that he was, he could hear it over all the music that the orchestra was playing.

"Fire!" Mose shouted with all his might. "Fire! Turn out, boys! Turn out!"

With that, every man in the place dropped whatever he was doing and ran for the nearest exit.

But by the time they got to the fire, it had already burned several blocks. It was the worst fire New York City had ever seen. Every single company in the city was there. Mose was up and down ladders rescuing people all through the night. But it was a losing battle. There just wasn't enough water, and the fire continued to burn out of control.

After a while it began to look completely hopeless. Mose sighed the saddest sigh ever sighed. Gotham would never be the same. From where he was, Mose could see the Hudson River at the edge of the island. It was all so sad. All that water and no way to get it to the fire.

Then suddenly Mose, lunatic that he was, got a crazy idea. A cockamamy, nutso, wacko idea. Although somehow the more he thought about it, the less nuts it seemed.

Without a moment to waste, Mose jumped down to the ground and grabbed the biggest shovel he could find. Then he rolled up his sleeves and started digging a hole in the general direction of New Jersey. Sykesey just looked at him. "Hey! This ain't no time for chasing groundhogs!" he said. "For crying out loud! What's the matter with you? The whole town's burning down!"

But by that time Mose was already underground and headed due west.

"Hey, Mose," Sykesey shouted, "Hey! Where ya going?"

"Where do ya think?" he shouted back. "To get water!" Well, that's all Mose had to say. He always kept his word, and Sykesey knew Mose would be back with water just like he said.

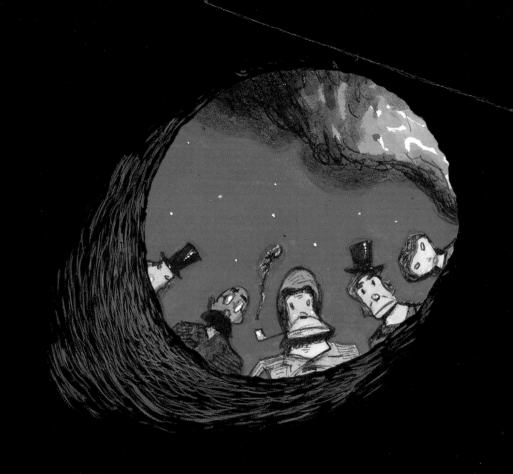

In a little while practically everybody in town was standing there looking into the hole, just waiting for Mose to reappear.

Suddenly there was a loud pop, followed by the sound a tidal wave might make, and then—*kaploosh!*—up shot Mose like a spooked fish, with the Hudson River right behind him.

Then, without wasting a second, Mose picked up Lady Washington all by himself and wedged her into the hole as tightly as possible.

"All right, everybody," he said. "We're going to have to work together. Hook every hose up to Lady Washington. Don't nobody crowd around! There's enough H-two-O for every one of you bums. And hurry it up, 'cause there ain't much time!"

Well, every company did as they were told, and the minute all the hoses were hooked up, Mose started pumping the brakes. He was moving so fast, it looked like a blur on top of a blur on top of a hallucination. But then, all of a sudden, it happened. Water began to shoot out of all those hoses at once. And the pressure in each hose was so unbelievable that it took every single man in each company just to keep 'em under control.

In fact, there was so much water coming out of those hoses that the fire didn't know which way to turn. It just freaked out. I guess you could say that the fire had met its match. Well, Mose continued pumping the brakes so fast that in no time at all every single flame and every last ember was extinguished. *Ba-da-bing!*

Just like that it was over. Mose had saved New York City.

The whole city erupted with cheers. "Hooray for Mose!" everyone shouted. "Hooray for the King of the Bowery! Mose has done it again!"

Now, of course this was true, but Mose was a very humble guy. He couldn't stand being the center of attention. "I'm just doing my duty," he said. You see, when you're as much of a hero as Mose was, you do stuff like drain the Hudson River without blinking. It's just what you do.

Well, people kept on cheering, and the noise was so loud that Mose had to scream his marriage proposal to Lize, who screamed back her answer, which was absolutely yes, definitely, no question about it, yes. And since everybody was already dressed for the occasion, they all went back up to the firehouse for the wedding and that was that. *Ba-da-bing!* Married.

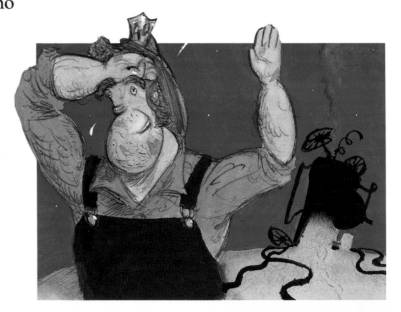

Oh, by the way, after Mose had
gotten through with the Hudson, it
took so long for it to fill back up that
for weeks you could just walk right
over to Jersey, which is not the
brightest idea in the world, but hey,
it's a free country. You want to go to
Jersey, go to Jersey. And as for the tunnel
he dug, it just kind of sat there for a while.

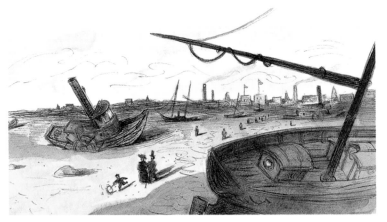

But after a couple of years somebody got the idea of putting train tracks down there—on account of it being nice and quiet and out of the way—and that's how subways came into being. Go figure. So I guess you could say Mose even had a hand in inventing the subways. But hey, nobody's perfect, am I right? Of course I am.